Disney The Never Girls

wedding wings

written by

Kiki Thorpe

Illustrated by

Jana Christy

A STEPPING STONE BOOK™

RANDOM HOUSE 🏠 NEW YORK

For Sienna and Audrey
—K.T.

For Johnny
—J.C.

Library of Congress Cataloging-in-Publication Data
Thorpe, Kiki.
Wedding wings / written by Kiki Thorpe ; illustrated by Jana Christy.
pages cm. — (Disney fairies) (The Never girls ; 5)
"A Stepping Stone book."
Summary: "The Never girls are going to a wedding, and Gabby is the flower girl.
When the fairies hear about it, they wish they could go, too. One little fairy hiding in
Gabby's basket couldn't cause too much trouble—right?"— Provided by publisher.
ISBN 978-0-7364-3077-7 (pbk.) — ISBN 978-0-7364-8141-0 (lib. bdg.)
ISBN 978-0-7364-3220-7 (ebook)
[1. Fairies—Fiction. 2. Magic—Fiction. 3. Weddings—Fiction. 4. Flower girls—Fiction.]
I. Christy, Jana, illustrator. II. Title.
PZ7.T3974We 2014
[Fic]—dc23

randomhouse.com/kids/disney
Printed in the United States of America
10 9 8 7 6 5 4 3 2 1

Never Land

Far away from the world we know, on the distant seas of dreams, lies an island called Never Land. It is a place full of magic, where mermaids sing, fairies play, and children never grow up. Adventures happen every day, and anything is possible.

There are two ways to reach Never Land. One is to find the island yourself. The other is for it to find you. Finding Never Land on your own takes a lot of luck and a pinch of fairy dust. Even then, you will only find the island if it wants to be found.

Every once in a while, Never Land drifts close to our world . . . so close a fairy's laugh slips through. And every once in an even longer while, Never Land opens its doors to a special few. Believing in magic and fairies from the bottom of your heart can make the extraordinary happen. If you suddenly hear tiny bells or feel a sea breeze where there is no sea, pay careful attention. Never Land may be close by. You could find yourself there in the blink of an eye.

One day, four special girls came to Never Land in just this way. This is their story.

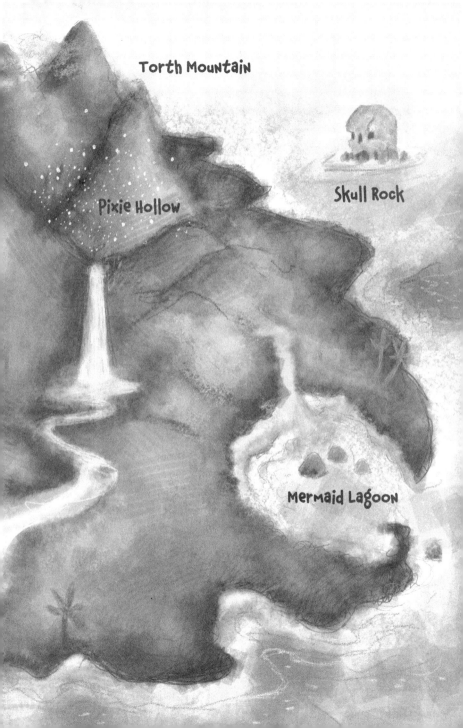

Torth Mountain

Pixie Hollow

Skull Rock

Mermaid Lagoon

Chapter 1

Gabby Vasquez hurried up the stairs to her room. She had news—the kind of fizzy, exciting news that wouldn't stay bottled up inside. She just had to tell someone about it!

In her bedroom, Gabby raced to the closet. She threw the door open wide, shouting, "Guess what, everyone?"

She stepped inside, pulling the door shut behind her. The closet was very dark, but it was a friendly sort of darkness. She could smell the sweet scent of orange blossoms and hear water trickling over rocks.

Gabby shuffled forward. Soon she saw a window of light. A moment later, she emerged into the sunshine of Pixie Hollow.

Hop-two-three. Gabby skipped from rock to rock, crossing Havendish Stream. She wriggled between two wild rosebushes on the far bank. Her costume fairy wings caught on a thorn. Gabby quickly checked to make sure the fabric hadn't ripped. Then she plunged ahead, stumbling a little in her hurry.

As she came over a small rise, she could see the Home Tree, the great maple where the Never fairies worked and lived. The fairies' golden glows shone among the leaves, making it seem as if the branches were filled with stars.

"Tink! Prilla! Everybody! Guess what?" Gabby shouted as she raced toward the tree.

On a high branch, the art-talent fairy Bess looked up from her painting. Prilla, the clapping-talent fairy, awoke from her doze in a cozy magnolia blossom. The pots-and-pans fairy Tinker Bell stuck her head out of her teakettle workshop. The garden fairy Rosetta set down her miniature gourd watering can. And Dulcie, a baking-talent fairy, dusted the flour from her hands. They all flew to the courtyard.

"What's going on?" Prilla asked as Gabby ran up to them, breathless.

Gabby bounced on her toes with excitement. "There's going to be a wedding," she announced. "And I'm the star!"

"A wedding?" cried Dulcie, wringing

3

her apron. "Why didn't anyone tell me? I haven't baked a thing!"

"Not here, silly," Gabby said. "At home. Our babysitter Julia is getting married, and I'm going to be the flower girl!"

"Is that anything like being a flower-talent fairy?" Rosetta asked.

"Kind of," said Gabby. "I'm in charge of all the flower magic. And I get to wear this special dress." She did a twirl so the fairies could admire her brand-new, pretty pink flower girl dress.

"It's lovely!" exclaimed Rosetta, who adored dresses of all kinds.

"I have this basket, too." Gabby held up a little basket with a bow tied around the handle. "And I throw flower petals. Like this." Gabby pretended to pull a handful of petals from the basket and throw them.

"Hmm." Rosetta frowned.

Gabby stopped. "What's the matter?"

"Why not practice with some *real* flowers?" Rosetta suggested. She plucked a bundle of daisies that were growing nearby and shook the petals into Gabby's basket.

Gabby threw a few of the petals. They plopped to the ground.

"Well, that's not very interesting," said Tink.

"Wouldn't it be nicer if the petals moved around a little?" suggested Bess. She dove into the basket and came up with an armful of petals. When she threw them into the air, they swirled like snowflakes.

Gabby gasped. "How did you do that?"

"It's easy. You just need a bit of fairy magic." Bess shook her wings over the basket. A sprinkle of fairy dust rained down on the petals. "Try it again."

This time the petals almost leaped from Gabby's hand. They fluttered in the air before drifting to the ground.

The fairies nodded happily.

"Oh yes!"

"Much nicer!"

"Just lovely."

Gabby smiled and threw another handful just to watch the petals swirl. "Can I have some fairy dust to take with me to the wedding tomorrow? Please?"

"I don't see why not," Tink said. She darted away. In a moment she was back with a little thimble bucket. It had a tight-fitting silver lid. "I made the lid myself," Tink said proudly. "You won't lose a speck of dust."

Gabby peeked inside and saw the shimmery fairy dust. "Thank you," she said, tucking the thimble into the pocket of her dress.

"I've heard of weddings, but I've never seen one," said Prilla. She traveled to the world of Clumsies—or humans—more than most fairies. "What are they like?"

"A wedding is when two people get married," Gabby told her. "They say 'I love you.' Then they give each other rings and everybody claps. And then . . ." Here, Gabby's knowledge of weddings became somewhat murky, but she continued, "Then they float away on a cloud and live happily ever after!"

"Very dramatic," Bess said approvingly.

"Will there be food at the wedding?" Dulcie asked.

"Yes! Really fancy food, like onion rings. And a cake this big!" Gabby stretched her hands up over her head. To the fairies, the cake seemed enormous.

"My!" Dulcie exclaimed.

"Will there be music and dancing?" Tinker Bell asked. "At fairy parties there's always dancing."

Gabby had no idea if there was dancing at a wedding. But her imagination had taken over now. "Everybody dances! And there are butterflies everywhere! And a chocolate waterfall!" Gabby spun on her toes, inspired by her own vision of how wonderful the wedding would be.

Prilla's freckled face took on a dreamy

look. "It sounds marvelous. I wish I could see it."

"You could come with me!" Gabby suggested.

"Gabby! Gabby?" a voice called out from the direction of Havendish Stream.

Everyone turned as Gabby's older sister, Mia, came into view. As soon as she spotted Gabby, her face darkened.

"Uh-oh," murmured Gabby.

"I knew it!" Mia said, charging over. "Gabby, you're not supposed to come here by yourself. Remember what happened last time?"

Gabby remembered. She'd gone to Never Land alone and gotten stuck there when the hole between their two worlds had briefly closed. After that, Gabby,

Mia, and their friends Kate McCrady and Lainey Winters had made a rule that they would always go to Never Land together—a rule that Gabby, in her excitement, had forgotten.

"It was just for a minute," she said. "I was going to come right back."

"She was telling us about the wedding," said Prilla, trying to be helpful.

Mia rolled her eyes. "Gabby hasn't stopped talking about it all week. It is exciting, though," she added. "It's our first wedding ever."

"But I'm the only flower girl," Gabby pointed out.

"That's just because you're the littlest. Flower girls are supposed to be little. I don't know why," Mia said. A tiny wrinkle formed between her eyebrows, but it was gone a moment later. "I wish we could stay," she told the fairies. "But it's bath time for Gabby, and Mami's looking for her. We'll be back soon, though. I promise."

Taking Gabby's hand, Mia began to walk toward the passage that led back to their world. "I can't believe you," she whispered to Gabby. "We only have one rule about Never Land and you've already broken it. And you made me break it, too. What will we tell Kate and Lainey?"

"We don't have to tell them," Gabby said quickly. She was sorry she'd forgotten their agreement. She didn't want Kate and Lainey to be upset. "You won't tell them, will you?"

"We'll see," said Mia.

They had almost reached Havendish Stream when Gabby stopped so suddenly she yanked her sister backward. "I almost forgot," she said. "I have to tell the fairies how to get to the wedding."

She started to turn around, but Mia stopped her. "The fairies can't come to the wedding," she said.

"But I want them to see me be a flower girl!" Gabby cried.

"There will be lots of people there tomorrow," Mia said. "What if someone sees them? No one can know about Pixie Hollow. It's our secret."

Mia let go of Gabby's hand as they crossed the stepping-stones in Havendish Stream. But at the foot of the hollow fig tree, Mia stopped. She knelt down so she was looking Gabby in the eye. "You can't

say a word about fairies or magic to anyone tomorrow. Promise?"

Gabby gazed back into her sister's
brown eyes. "Okay," she said. "I promise."

＊

After the girls left, the fairies went
back to what they'd been doing. Rosetta
flew off to water the lilies. Tinker Bell
returned to her workshop. Dulcie, inspired by Gabby's description, headed to
the kitchen to try her hand at a seven-
layer thimble cake.

Bess flew back to her matchstick easel.
She had been working on a painting of
a dew-covered spiderweb. The dewdrops
were so plump and glistening they seemed
about to roll right off the canvas.

Bess had been proud of her painting.

But now, as she picked up her paintbrush, it struck her as boring. *So ordinary,* she thought. *So . . . fairyish.*

Her thoughts strayed to Gabby's description of the wedding. "Now, that would be an exciting painting," Bess said to herself.

"What's that?" asked Prilla as she flew by.

"I was just thinking about Gabby's wedding," said Bess.

"That's funny. So was I," said Prilla.

"I was thinking I might make a painting of it," Bess said.

"Oh, Bess, you should. That would be almost as good as being there," Prilla said. Bess's paintings were magical that way.

Bess took out the pencil she kept tucked behind her ear. She began to make a sketch on a little piece of birch bark. She drew two Clumsies as tall as palm trees—all Clumsies looked like giants to Bess. But then her imagination failed her.

"What are their clothes made from? The Clumsies, I mean," Bess wondered. "A fairy gown would be sewn from lily petals, or maybe a rose. But that would never fit a Clumsy."

"I don't know," Prilla replied. "I've never thought about where Clumsies get their clothes."

"Speaking of flowers, what do the Clumsies do with them?" Bess asked. "Clumsies are too big to rest in a magnolia when they get tired of dancing. And how do they dance without wings, anyway? Their feet would never leave the ground! What kind of dancing is that?"

"They must look very silly," Prilla agreed.

Bess glanced at her sketch and frowned. "You're lucky, Prilla," she said. "You could just blink over to the mainland and see the wedding for yourself." Prilla had the special ability to travel to the world of Clumsies by blinking. She was the only fairy in Pixie Hollow with that talent.

"I guess I could," Prilla said. "But we haven't been properly invited."

"Oh, right," said Bess.

"You could go, too. You could fly through the hole in the old fig tree to get to the girls' world," Prilla pointed out.

"I could," said Bess. "But like you said, we haven't been invited. Besides, I wouldn't know where to go when I got there."

"I suppose that's true," Prilla said.

The two were quiet for a moment, thinking their own thoughts.

"It *would* be fun to be a gnat on the wall, though, wouldn't it?" Bess murmured. "Just to see the wedding, without anyone knowing you're there?"

Prilla said something in reply, but Bess wasn't listening. She was gazing off in the direction of Havendish Stream—and the old fig tree.

Chapter 2

The next morning, Gabby stood in the doorway of her bedroom. Her pink flower girl dress was zipped up and buttoned. Her hair was brushed, her shoes were buckled, and her wings were on straight. She was ready for her big day.

But where was everyone else?

Gabby tiptoed across the hall to Mia's room and peeked in. Mia stood before the mirror, brushing her long hair. Lainey sat on the bed, and Kate was fidgeting with her skirt.

"I still don't understand why I have to dress up," Kate grumbled. "Julia's the one getting married. Not me."

Mia turned from the mirror. "You just don't like wearing dresses because they show your knees," she pointed out.

Kate looked down at her knees. They were covered with scrapes from soccer and softball and many adventures in Never Land. She frowned and tugged the hem of her skirt lower. "I don't like wearing dresses, period. You can't climb trees in a dress."

"You *could*," Lainey pointed out. "But someone might see your underwear."

"Exactly!" cried Kate.

"No one is going to be climbing trees today," said Mia. "It's a wedding! Anyway, I *like* getting dressed up." She picked up a flowered barrette and clipped it in her hair.

As she admired herself in the mirror, Mia caught sight of Gabby peeping in the door. Mia sighed. "Will you ever learn to knock?" she asked.

Gabby knocked, then stepped into the room.

"Gabby, you look very nice," said Lainey.

"Just like a flower fairy," Kate agreed. "Too bad the fairies can't see you."

Gabby cast a worried glance at her sister. Would she tell Kate and Lainey about her visit to Pixie Hollow?

Mia frowned but didn't say anything.

"Are we leaving soon?" Gabby asked.

"I don't know," Mia replied. "Go find Mami and ask her."

Gabby sighed and wandered down the hall to her parents' room. She stood in the doorway. Her parents were rushing around getting ready.

"Have you seen my green tie?" Gabby's father called. He still had a blob of shaving cream under his chin.

"Look in the closet," Gabby's mother said. "Now, where did I leave my purse?" She brushed past Gabby, trailing perfume.

"When are we leaving?" Gabby asked.

"Soon," her mother promised.

Gabby went back down the hall, scuffing her feet. She hated waiting. It seemed as if they would never get to the wedding!

At the end of the hall was a small window that overlooked the backyard. Gabby pressed her nose to the glass, gazing at the garden below. She could see the flower bed where she'd first met Prilla.

Was something moving among the marigolds? Gabby squinted. She thought she saw a flash of golden light among the orange and red flowers.

"All ready to go?" asked her father.

Gabby whirled around. Her parents, along with Mia, Kate, and Lainey, were in the hallway. "What are you looking at?" her father asked, coming to stand by her.

"Nothing, Papi. Just Bingo," Gabby said, referring to the family cat. Quickly, she stepped away from the window.

"Oh, sweetie," said her mother, looking at her closely for the first time. "You can't wear those to the wedding."

Gabby glanced down at her clothes. She wondered what her mother meant. Was there something wrong with her dress or her shoes?

"Julia is expecting a flower girl, not a fairy. You'll have to leave your wings at home," said her mother.

She might as well have asked Gabby to leave her arms at home. "Mami, no!" Gabby cried, clutching the straps on her shoulders.

Her mother knelt down next to her. "I know you love your wings," she said. "But this is Julia's special day. Can you do it for her?"

Gabby looked over at Mia, Kate, and

26

Lainey. Mia gave her a tiny nod, as if to say, "You can do it."

Gabby turned back to her mother. "Okay," she agreed with a sigh.

Slowly, she slipped one arm out of the straps, then the other. Her back felt bare where the wings had been. "I'm going to put them away," she said.

In her room, Gabby carefully folded her wings and placed them on the bed. She didn't feel quite as excited as she had before. Without her wings, being a flower girl lost some of its magic.

Gabby heard a tiny rattle behind her, like a key turning in a lock. She looked around. The sound had come from her closet.

Gabby watched as a teeny head poked out of the keyhole. Two small arms emerged next. After a bit of wriggling, a pair of iridescent wings followed.

The fairy flew into the room. She had a long, messy ponytail and a smudge of paint on her cheek. It was Bess.

When Bess saw Gabby, her face lit up. "You're here! So I'm not too late!"

"Too late for what?" asked Gabby.

"The wedding, of course!" Bess said. "I'd like to come with you. If you don't mind, that is."

Gabby's heart lifted. A fairy had come to see her in the wedding! Her excitement returned. "Yay! But— Oh!" Suddenly, Gabby remembered her promise to Mia.

"What's wrong?" Bess asked.

If Gabby told Bess what Mia had said,

the fairy might decide to go home.

I promised Mia I wouldn't say anything about fairies or Pixie Hollow, Gabby thought. *But I never said I wouldn't* bring *a fairy.*

"You can come," she told Bess at last. "But you can't let anyone see you."

"That's all right. I can hide in your basket," Bess said. She flew into the flower basket. Gabby covered her with a tissue

from a box next to her bed. And not a moment too soon, for just then they heard a knock on the door.

Mia, Kate, and Lainey walked in. "Are you okay, Gabby?" Lainey asked.

Gabby stood up straight. "I am now."

"Mami and Papi say we'll be late if we don't leave right away." Mia's eyes darted to the closet door. "You didn't go to Never Land, did you?" she whispered.

"Of course not," Gabby said. And squeezing past Mia and the other girls, she headed for the stairs.

Chapter 3

City Park was the biggest park in town. It had a duck pond, a carousel, and a little grassy hill where people went to fly kites. There were lots of paths for walking or riding bikes and benches where you could sit and rest in the shade.

The wedding was taking place near the pond, which was ringed with giant willow trees. Gabby saw rows and rows of white chairs facing the water. A great white tent had been set up on the grass. A few people

scurried around inside it, laying silver-
ware on tables and putting out food.

"Isn't this a lovely place for a wedding!"
her mother said.

Gabby swallowed hard. It all looked
much bigger and more grown-up than she
had imagined—big, and a little scary. She
wriggled her shoulders, feeling the empty
space on her back where her wings should
have been.

Bess poked her head out from Gabby's
basket. "Are we there yet?"

"Not now, Bess," Gabby whispered. She
pulled the tissue back over the fairy, just
as Lainey walked up next to her. Lainey
had her sweater bundled in her arms, as if
she were carrying a package.

"Are you sure you're okay? About your
wings, I mean," she said.

32

Gabby nodded. She held her hand over the basket so Lainey couldn't peek inside.

"We'd better find someone and let them know we're here," Mrs. Vasquez said.

At that moment, a woman in a pink suit came striding toward them. She carried a clipboard in the crook of her elbow.

"Is this our flower girl?" she exclaimed. She checked her clipboard, adding, "Gabriela Vasquez?"

"It's Gabby, not Gabriela," Gabby said shyly.

"Aren't you cute," the woman replied. She made a little checkmark on her clipboard, then turned to Gabby's parents. "I'm Amanda Cork, the wedding planner. I'm here to make sure everything is perfect."

"Can we go say hi to Julia?" Mia asked.

"Of course not!" the wedding planner exclaimed. "A bride should never be disturbed when she's dressing for her big day—"

"Is that Mia and Gabby I hear?" a familiar voice called. "And Lainey and Kate?"

The girls turned. Not far from the pond was a little building known as the clubhouse. Julia's smiling face peeked out of the door.

"Julia!" the girls cried, rushing to her.

When Gabby saw her babysitter, her mouth opened in surprise. Instead of her usual jeans and T-shirt, Julia was dressed in a long gown made of white lace.

"You look like a princess!" Gabby exclaimed.

"You look really pretty," Lainey agreed.

"I love your dress," Mia gushed.

"Yeah, it really covers your knees," added Kate.

Julia laughed. "Thank you," she said. "You all look very nice, too."

Ms. Cork hurried up behind them. "Are these girls bothering you?" she asked.

"Of course not," said Julia. "They were just saying hello."

"There's time for all that later." Ms. Cork sniffed. "The wedding starts in"— she checked her watch—"fifty-six minutes. You should finish getting ready! I'm sure you girls can find some way to amuse yourselves. Not you, Gabby," the wedding planner added as the girls started to walk away. "You can stay. I have some flower girl instructions to give you."

As the other girls left, Gabby looked around the clubhouse. Inside was a cozy room with a sofa, a dressing table, and a full-length mirror.

Gabby pointed to a long piece of gauzy fabric draped over a hanger on the closet door. "What's that?"

"That's my veil," Julia replied. "Isn't it pretty?"

Gabby nodded. The veil cascaded in lovely, loose folds. It reminded her of a waterfall. She wondered how it felt—

"No touching!" Ms. Cork exclaimed. "Your hands might be dirty."

Gabby jerked her hand away. "They aren't dirty," she said, but she clasped her hands behind her back anyway.

Gabby waited for her flower girl

instructions. But the wedding planner started talking to Julia. Something about place mats—or was it place cards? Gabby was having trouble following the conversation.

Suddenly, she realized Julia and Ms. Cork were heading for the door. "Wait here, Gabby. We'll be right back," Julia said. The door closed behind them.

As soon as they were gone, Bess fluttered out of Gabby's basket. "I thought they'd never leave! I'm going outside to look around."

"Are you going far?" Gabby asked, worried. She was a little scared of Ms. Cork, and she didn't want to be left alone. "Don't you want to see me be a flower girl?"

"I do!" Bess said. "I just want to take a

peek. I'll be back in a firefly's flash." With a little wave, Bess flew out the window.

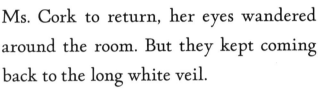

Gabby sighed. As she waited for Julia and Ms. Cork to return, her eyes wandered around the room. But they kept coming back to the long white veil.

The filmy fabric looked a bit like her own fairy wings. It looked . . . magical. Gabby reached out a finger and stroked the veil, forgetting that she wasn't supposed to touch it.

As she ran her finger along the edges, the veil suddenly slid off the hanger. It landed in a heap at her feet. Gabby gasped. She glanced around to make sure no one had seen, then quickly gathered up the fabric.

She meant to put it right back. But once the veil was in her arms, Gabby couldn't resist the urge to try it on.

Just for a second, she told herself. *No one will know.*

Gabby tried to put the veil on her head, but it kept sliding back to the floor. At last she discovered two little combs attached to the corners. She pushed the combs into her hair and pretended she was walking down the aisle.

But the veil was too long. She kept tripping over the end.

"Oopsie!" Gabby said as she stepped on it once, then again. "Whoops!"

At last, by wadding the trailing veil into a ball, Gabby managed to carry it over to the mirror. But when she let the veil flow down, it didn't look pretty or princessy anymore. Instead of falling in long, lovely folds, the fabric was wrinkly and crumpled. There was a smudgy mark in one corner. Looking closer, Gabby saw that it was a footprint.

A sick, scared feeling churned in her stomach. *Maybe if I hurry and put it back, no one will notice anything is wrong,* she thought.

But Gabby had another problem. She couldn't reach the hanger. It was too high over her head.

Where's Bess? Gabby thought. *She could use magic to put it back— Oh!*

Suddenly, she remembered the thimbleful of fairy dust in her pocket. Gabby knew fairy dust could make things fly and float. Maybe it could lift the veil for her.

Gabby pulled out the thimble and sprinkled some dust on the veil. "Abracadabra," she said, for good measure. "Go back to your hanger."

At first, nothing happened. Then, slowly, the veil rose into the air. Gabby sighed with relief.

But the veil kept on rising. It floated past Gabby, past the hanger, and headed for the open window.

The veil flapped like the wings of a great white bird, then soared outside and disappeared.

Chapter 4

Bess hovered beneath the canopy of the big white tent. Below her, Clumsies were briskly preparing for the celebration. They were setting tables, folding napkins, and carrying platters of food.

Bess marveled at the scene. The round tables reminded her of the tables in the Home Tree dining room—except they were built for giants!

She swooped down to look at one of the place settings. The bowl was big enough for her to bathe in. The teaspoon was the size of a garden fairy's shovel. Fifteen fairies could sit comfortably around the dinner plate.

Bess darted out of the way as a Clumsy set down a vase filled with flowers. She didn't worry about being spotted. Most grown-ups didn't believe in fairies, and fairies could only be seen by Clumsies who believed. But she did need to take care not to get squashed.

When the Clumsy was gone, Bess poked around the flower arrangement. She undid an artfully folded napkin to see how it was done. She made faces at her reflection in a soup spoon. *How am I ever going to decide what to put into my painting?* she wondered. There was so much to look at—and everything was huge! She'd need a canvas the size of the Home Tree to fit it all in.

Bess held up her thumb and forefinger. She looked through the window they made, trying to frame the scene in her mind.

Bess gasped. Through the makeshift frame, she saw two tiny figures on the other side of the tent. They looked like fairies!

"Fly with you!" Bess swooped toward them, calling out the fairy greeting.

The fairies didn't respond. They didn't even move. As she landed, Bess saw they weren't fairies at all, but little statues of a man and woman.

Bess walked around the statues, studying them. The woman wore a white dress, and the man was in a dark suit. The carved faces were blank and expressionless. Bess couldn't imagine what they were for.

I'll have to ask Gabby, she thought. As a matter of fact, it was time she found her friend.

But as she fluttered her wings to leave, Bess found that her feet were stuck. She was sinking into the ground, which, actually, was not ground at all but—

"Frosting!" Bess exclaimed. She was up to her ankles in it. Now she realized that she was standing on a giant cake. Her tiny footprints covered the top tier.

"Oh, smudge!" cried Bess. She tried to swipe one of the footprints away with her paintbrush. But she only made a bigger smear. "Double smudge!"

Maybe I can turn the footprints into a pattern, she thought. *That way they'll look like they're there on purpose.*

Bess began to walk around the top of the cake, weaving in and out. It was slow going. The frosting was as thick and heavy as mud. It took effort to drag each foot out. But at last she managed to create a beautiful spiral pattern around the statues.

She stepped back to admire her work. "Not bad, if I do say so my— Ahhh!"

The edge of cake she'd been standing on gave way suddenly. Bess slid down in an avalanche of frosting. She bounced off the second tier, rolled to the first, then fell onto the table.

She groaned and sat up. Looking back

at the cake, she saw a Bess-sized track running down the side.

"Blasted broken brushes! How am I going to fix *that*?" she exclaimed.

But before she could even think of fixing the cake, she needed to get cleaned up. She was sticky with frosting.

Somewhere nearby, Bess could hear the sound of water trickling. She flew toward it, hoping to find a place to wash.

Bess followed the sound to a table. There were bowls piled high with strawberries, and right in the middle was a giant fountain. It flowed with something thick, brown, and sweet-smelling.

"Chocolate!" Bess exclaimed. She had found the chocolate waterfall!

Bess hesitated. She really needed to get cleaned up. But if there was one thing

Bess loved almost as much as painting, it was chocolate.

"I'll just take a teensy taste," she told herself. "Then I'll be on my way." Bess climbed onto the edge of the fountain.

At that moment, a Clumsy set a bowl of strawberries down right next to her. Startled, Bess lost her balance—

Sploosh! She fell up to her waist into the chocolate.

"Ugh!" Bess stood on her tiptoes, trying to hold her wings above the thick brown liquid. If they went under, she'd never get out!

She tried to lift her legs. *Gloop.* The chocolate pulled one of her shoes right off.

Bess reached into the chocolate. She stuck her arm in all the way up to the elbow. But she couldn't find her shoe. She tried with her other arm. She thought she felt it with the tip of her finger. She stretched her arms as far as she could until she finally grabbed hold of the shoe.

Bess stood up with a gasp, wiping chocolate from her chin. She was covered from neck to toe. Luckily, she'd managed to keep her wings dry. Now she fluttered them hard to pull herself out.

She landed on the table, making a big chocolate splatter.

"Ugh! What a mess!" How was she going to clean herself up now?

A loud scream made her jump. "That's the biggest bug I've ever seen!" a Clumsy exclaimed.

"It's horrible!" said another.

Bess glanced around nervously, looking for the big, horrible bug. Instead, she saw two Clumsies holding covered platters. They were both staring down at her.

They can't be looking at me, Bess thought. *Grown-up Clumsies can't see fairies, unless . . . Uh-oh!*

Bess suddenly realized they *could* see her. Covered in chocolate, she was no longer invisible. Now she looked like a big, ugly brown bug!

"Squish it!" one of the Clumsies said. The next thing Bess saw was a huge silver lid coming toward her.

chapter 5

Outside, Gabby hurried across the grass toward the rows of white chairs. Guests had started to arrive. The seats were beginning to fill with people.

"Bess?" Gabby whispered. She crept along the aisle. She peeked under the chairs, but all she saw were feet. Where could the fairy be?

"What are you looking for?" asked a voice behind her.

Gabby jumped and spun around. A boy her age was standing there. He was dressed in a little blue suit with a white bow tie. In his hands, he held a small satin pillow.

"I was trying to find my friend," Gabby said, staring at the pillow. She wondered what it was for. Was the boy planning to take a nap?

"Why were you looking under the chairs?" the boy asked.

Gabby remembered her promise to Mia about not mentioning fairies. "I thought I saw a butterfly," she fibbed.

"I caught a butterfly yesterday," the boy said. "It was yellow and blue. I put it in my bug hotel."

"What's a bug hotel?" Gabby asked.

"It's this jar with holes in the lid. When you catch a bug, you put it in there. The bug can have a drink of water and some leaves to eat. Maybe it can take a nap. Then you have to let the bug go, so it can go home to its family."

"Can I see it?" Gabby asked.

The boy shrugged. "Nah. It's at home."

Gabby hoped the boy would go away now. How could she find Bess with him standing right there?

A hand suddenly clamped down on her shoulder. "There you are, Gabriela!" Ms. Cork exclaimed. "I've been looking all over for you."

Fear seized Gabby. Had Ms. Cork found out what she'd done?

But the wedding planner didn't look

angry. She held up a little box. "These are your rose petals," she said, emptying the contents into Gabby's basket. "You're to sprinkle them when you walk down the aisle. Can you do that?"

Gabby nodded, clutching the basket. She hoped Ms. Cork would leave now, too, so she could go back to looking for the veil and Bess.

But Ms. Cork seemed to be in no hurry. "Let's practice," she said. "Take a handful of petals and sprinkle them. Sprinkle them *gaily*!"

Gabby lobbed a fistful of petals into the air. Most of them landed on Ms. Cork's feet.

"A little less force next time," she said, shaking off her shoes. "I see you've met Daniel. He's our ring bearer. He'll be

going down the aisle right in front of you, so all you have to do is follow him. Can you do that?"

Gabby nodded again. She wished Ms. Cork would stop talking to her as if she were a baby.

At that moment, a shout came from the tent, followed by a loud clatter.

Ms. Cork frowned. "I'd better go see what that's about," she said, to Gabby's relief. "Don't go running off anywhere. The wedding will be starting very soon." She bustled away.

"I don't like her," said Daniel.

"Me either," said Gabby. "Okay, I'll see you later—"

"Wait," said Daniel. "I want to show you something."

He led Gabby over to a row of white chairs. Tucked beneath one of the chairs was a beautiful kite.

"It's nice," said Gabby. The kite was shaped like a dragonfly, with purple wings and big green eyes.

"Dragonflies are my favorite bugs," he said. "My mom and dad said we can go fly

the kite as soon as the wedding is over. You can come if you want."

"Okay," said Gabby. She was starting to think Daniel was nice.

Just then, she saw something over Daniel's shoulder that made her heart pound. The veil was drifting across the lawn. It floated past like a ghost. Then it disappeared around the side of the tent.

Gabby knew there was no time to find Bess now. She'd have to catch the veil herself!

As she ran after it, she heard Daniel call, "Hey, where are you going?"

Behind the tent, the veil was rolling across the grass like a big white tumbleweed. She tried to catch it, but it was always just out of reach.

Then the veil became snagged on a

bush. Gabby lunged for it. But as her fingertips brushed the fabric, a gust of wind snatched the veil away. It soared up . . . up . . . up. One end flapped, as if waving good-bye.

Gabby collapsed onto the grass. She blinked back tears of frustration. She was never going to be fast enough to catch a magical flying veil. Unless . . .

Gabby reached into her pocket and found the thimble bucket. There was still a tiny bit of fairy dust clinging to the sides. Maybe it was enough.

Gabby had only had one flying lesson in Pixie Hollow. She tried to remember how it worked. *Think happy thoughts and kick your feet*—that was it, wasn't it? Or were you *not* supposed to kick?

There wasn't time to waste. She'd have

to figure it out as she went. She sprinkled the remaining dust over herself.

Gabby felt a tingly feeling, like bubbles rising in a soda bottle. The next thing she knew, her feet were lifting off the ground.

chapter 6

Not far away, on the buffet table, Bess was running for her life.

Wham! A massive serving spoon crashed down. It missed her by a hair. Bess changed direction in time to see a fist holding a crumpled napkin swing toward her.

With a flutter of wings, Bess dodged it. She zigzagged across the table, searching for an exit.

If only she could fly! But the Clumsies were always just above her, blocking her way. They filled the air with their shouts and their flailing arms. Bess couldn't find a clear space for takeoff.

She scurried between two platters of fruit. It was becoming tougher and tougher to run. The chocolate that covered her was hardening. It formed a thick brown shell over her whole body. Her hands felt like they were inside chocolate mittens. Chocolate boots encased her feet.

Slam! A hand swung at her, upending a bowl of fruit. Strawberries tumbled everywhere. In the space where the bowl had been, Bess saw an opening. She ran toward it, jumping over berries that rolled into her path.

As she reached the edge of the table, a Clumsy loomed over her. He held two platter lids in his hands. He clashed the

lids together like cymbals just as Bess leaped.

She felt the lids whoosh past her—so close they grazed the tips of her wings. A second later, she tumbled into the grass below.

Bess didn't waste a moment. She fluttered her wings and flew away. She had to find Gabby!

Outside the tent, Bess looked around.

She spotted the small building where she'd left the little girl.

The door was shut tight, but Bess flew up to the window. She clung to the sill, peeking in. Julia, the girls' babysitter, was talking to another Clumsy.

"I don't know what could have happened to it," Julia was saying.

"Well, it must be around here somewhere. Veils don't just fly away on their own," the woman replied.

Bess looked all around the room. There was no sign of Gabby. She started to turn from the window.

Suddenly, two hands closed around her. "Gotcha!" someone cried.

Bess fluttered and fought, trying to free herself. But the hands cupped her, holding tight. Through the cracks between the Clumsy's fingers, an eyeball peeped in at her.

"Ooh! What kind of bug are you?" said a boy's voice.

"I'm not a bug!" Bess cried. If the boy heard her, he gave no sign. He shoved Bess into a little paper bag and closed it.

"Let me out!" Bess kicked at the side of the bag.

"Are you hungry, bug? Here are some leaves to eat." The boy opened the bag and thrust a leaf down at Bess. "When we get home you can have lots more."

The bag closed again. Curled in her tiny prison, Bess sighed. She thought about how she'd ended up in this spot. *Why didn't I just stay in Gabby's basket?* she asked herself.

She thought of Gabby in her pink dress. She'd been so excited for Bess to watch her in the wedding. Surely she was wondering where Bess was.

She probably thinks I forgot all about her, Bess thought miserably. *And what's going to happen to me now?*

Bess realized she hadn't been completely honest with Gabby. Of course she'd wanted to see Gabby be a flower girl. But she'd been more concerned about making her painting.

Bess's stomach rumbled, as if it, too, were sorry to find itself in such a fix. She *was* hungry. She hadn't had a thing to eat since she left Pixie Hollow.

Bess looked down at her chocolate-covered hands, her chocolate-covered arms, and her chocolate-covered legs. There was nothing she could do about Gabby right now. But there was one thing she *could* do.

She broke off a bit of chocolate and began to nibble.

Chapter 7

"Is it time yet?" asked Kate.

Mia, Kate, and Lainey were lingering near the rows of white chairs. In the half hour since they'd left Gabby with Julia, they'd walked all the way around the pond—twice. They'd made bets on the flavor of wedding cake. (Kate guessed chocolate. Lainey guessed vanilla. Mia guessed lemon with raspberry cream.) They'd even hidden beneath one of the big willow trees to spy on guests as they arrived. They had run out of ideas for things to do, and *still* the wedding hadn't begun.

Lainey shifted her bundled sweater to her other arm, then checked her watch. "The wedding doesn't start for another twenty minutes," she said.

"Why are you carrying your sweater around like that? Why don't you put it on?" Kate asked irritably. Boredom always made her cranky.

Lainey tucked the sweater more firmly under her arm. "I'm not cold," she replied with a shrug.

"Let's go sit down," Mia suggested. "Look, there are Mami and Papi. We can sit next to them."

"Where do you think Gabby is?" Lainey

asked as they made their way over to the seats.

"Having fun with Julia, probably," Mia replied. Her brow furrowed. "It's just not fair."

"What's not fair?" asked Kate.

"I always wanted to be a flower girl, but I never got the chance," Mia said. "And now I'm too old. It doesn't seem fair that Gabby gets to be one. Isn't the point of being a big sister getting to do everything first?"

"I think you would have been a great flower girl," Lainey said.

"I know." Mia sighed.

"Oh!" Lainey gasped and stood up from her chair.

"What is it?" asked Kate.

"I saw a fairy! There, by the bushes," Lainey whispered.

The other girls looked to where she was pointing. "I don't see anything. Are you sure?" Mia asked.

"Yes . . . well, no. Not completely sure," Lainey replied. "I only saw a flash, but it looked like a fairy."

"What would a fairy be doing here?" Kate asked.

Mia bit her lip. "You don't suppose they would have followed us, do you?"

"Nah," said Kate. "Why would they come without telling us?"

"I guess you're right," Mia said, relaxing a little. "Maybe you just imagined it, Lainey."

"I wouldn't mind if it was a fairy, though," Kate added. "It would be more exciting than all of this waiting around. In fact, I wish we were in Pixie Hollow right now!"

"Kate! Shh! Not so loud," Mia whispered. She glanced over at her parents to see if they'd heard. But they were busy chatting with some other wedding guests.

At that moment, she saw a flash of pink out of the corner of her eye. Something was rising over the top of the tent.

Mia gasped. It was Gabby! The little girl was floating through the air like a lost balloon.

Mia opened her mouth to shout, then thought better of it. She jerked back around and stared straight ahead, trying to think what to do.

"What's wrong?" asked Kate.

"Don't look now," Mia muttered.

Of course, that only made Kate and Lainey want to look. They twisted around in their seats.

"Holy guacamole!" said Kate.

"I said not to look," Mia hissed. But she had turned around again, too.

Gabby paddled the air, as if she were swimming. One hand still clutched her little basket. Her legs kicked helplessly behind her.

She drifted over a crowd of wedding guests who were standing on the grass in front of the tent. None of them noticed the little girl above their heads.

"Don't look up. Don't look up," Mia pleaded.

Then Gabby started to sink. She was headed right for a woman's large sunhat.

"She's going to crash!" Kate cried.

Lainey put her hands over her glasses. "I can't watch."

At the last second, Gabby paddled back up through the air. Mia, Kate, and Lainey watched as she sailed over the trees around the pond and disappeared from view.

The girls exchanged glances. Mia turned to her mother. In the calmest voice she could manage, she said, "Mami, we'll be right back."

"Where are you going?" her mother asked in surprise. "The ceremony is about to start."

"I have to go to the bathroom," Mia told her.

Her mother sighed. "All right. But hurry back."

The girls sprang from their chairs and raced in the direction Gabby had gone.

Down by the pond, it was shady and quiet. A light breeze stirred the leaves of the willow trees.

"I don't see her," Lainey whispered as they walked around the edge of the pond. The girls kept their voices low so none of the other wedding guests would hear.

"I can't believe Gabby was flying!" Kate said. She began to giggle.

Lainey started to giggle, too. "And at Julia's wedding!"

Mia frowned. "It's not funny, you guys. Remember the first time we flew in Pixie Hollow? We all ended up in the stream."

The girls looked at the lily-covered pond. "You don't think Gabby fell in, do you?" asked Lainey.

"No. We would have heard the splash," said Kate.

"Look!" Mia pointed at a nearby willow. Its leaves were trembling violently. Tipping their heads back, the girls could see Gabby high in the branches.

"Gabby!" Mia said in her loudest whisper. "Get down from there *right now*!"

Gabby didn't respond. She was thrashing around in the leaves. The girls could see something long and white tangled in the branches.

"What's she doing?" Lainey asked.

"Do you hear me, Gabby?" Mia said. "You'd better come down now, or else."

"I can't," Gabby replied. Her voice sounded small and scared.

"Why don't you fly down?" Mia asked.

"I can't let go." Gabby peered through the leaves at them. She was clinging to a branch with one hand, as if to keep from blowing away. Her arm held tight to her flower girl basket, and her other hand clutched a piece of long white fabric. The veil fluttered as if it were being blown by a breeze.

"I think she's stuck," said Kate.

"I *told* her no magic at the wedding," Mia said. "She never listens!"

"We can't leave her up there," Lainey said.

"I know." Mia turned to Kate. "Remember what I said about no one climbing trees at the wedding?"

"Yeah," said Kate.

"Well," Mia said, "I take it back."

chapter 8

"Can you see anybody coming?" asked Kate as she scrambled up onto a low branch of the willow.

"All clear," said Lainey, who was standing lookout.

"Good," Kate said, climbing higher. "I don't want anyone to see my underwear."

Mia was standing beneath the tree, holding out her arms in case someone fell. "No one is going to care about your underwear if we get caught," she explained.

"All the same, I wish I'd worn pants," said Kate. She pulled herself onto another branch with ease.

When she reached the branch where Gabby was clinging, Kate inched out as far as she could. "Give me your hand."

Gabby shook her head.

"Don't be scared," said Kate. "Just let go of that curtain, or whatever it is."

Gabby shook her head again, harder this time.

"Well, you're going to have to fly down. Do you have any more fairy dust?" Kate asked. "Then we could both fly down together!"

"I used it all up," Gabby said.

"It figures," Kate said with a sigh. "I'll

guide you, then. I'll need both hands to climb, so hold on to my shirt."

Gabby let go of the tree branch and took hold of the back of Kate's shirt. Kate began to climb down, pulling Gabby along with her. "Stop kicking, Gabby. You're throwing me off balance," she complained.

"I'm not doing anything," Gabby said.

"Then what's wiggling?" Kate asked.

It was the veil, of course. It had begun to flap again. Just as Kate reached the lowest branch, it broke free of Gabby's grasp and sailed into the air. The force of it tugged Gabby and Kate out of the tree.

Gabby landed on Kate, Kate landed on Mia, and Mia landed on the ground. Gabby's basket rolled away. The rose petals scattered.

"My petals!" Gabby wailed. All the tears she'd been holding back since losing the veil flooded her eyes.

The other girls gathered around her. Lainey gave the little girl's shoulder a comforting pat. "They're only flower petals, Gabby," she said. "At least no one got hurt."

"Not *very* hurt, anyway." Mia rubbed her bruised backside.

"I wish I was never a flower girl!" Gabby sobbed. "Ms. Cork is going to be mad about the petals. And Julia is going to be mad when she finds out I lost her veil—"

Mia raised a hand. "Hold on. Did you just say you *lost* Julia's veil?"

"Maybe you'd better explain," said Kate.

So Gabby told them everything, from her sneaky-quick visit to Pixie Hollow to bringing Bess to the wedding in her flower basket to losing the veil out of Julia's dressing-room window. By the time she was done explaining, Gabby's tears had dried. In truth, it felt good to finally tell someone else about everything that had gone wrong.

To Gabby's relief, Kate and Lainey weren't mad about her breaking their Pixie Hollow rule. And when she heard about Bess, Mia only rubbed her forehead and said, "Oh, Gabby."

"I *knew* I saw a fairy!" Lainey exclaimed.

"What am I going to do?" Gabby asked. "I lost the veil *and* Bess."

"We'll help you get the veil back," Mia said. "As for Bess, I'm sure she's wondering where you are right now. The wedding is going to start any minute."

"How are we going to get all the way up there?" Lainey asked. They could see the veil flying over the meadow, swooping among the kites in the sky.

"Gabby could fly," Kate suggested. "Although she's not so great at steering."

"We can't risk it. What if someone saw her?" said Mia.

Gabby gazed toward the colorful kites. "I have an idea!" she said.

*

A few minutes later, Gabby was high up in the sky. She could see the whole park stretched out below her—the ball fields, the carousel, the pond, and the big white tent.

91

How much fun it was to fly! Clinging to Daniel's kite, Gabby turned a little loop. She was using the kite to hide behind. Anyone passing by would think the other girls were just out having fun on a sunny summer day.

The girls had found the kite in Daniel's hiding spot. Gabby had wanted to ask if she

could borrow it, but she didn't know where Daniel was and there wasn't a moment to lose. She hoped he wouldn't mind that she got to fly his kite before he did.

A sharp tug on the kite string made Gabby look down. On the ground below, she saw Mia making a "hurry up" gesture.

The veil was just ahead of Gabby. It turned a loop-de-loop in the wind. Gabby steered the kite toward it. The veil dodged right. Gabby followed on the kite. The veil zoomed down. Gabby stayed on its tail.

At last, it was within reach. Gabby snatched up an edge of the fabric. As soon as she had it, Kate began to reel her in. Gabby landed with the veil clasped in her arms.

"You did it!" Mia exclaimed, giving her a hug.

Faint music floated from the direction of the pond. Lainey checked her watch. "It's almost noon! The wedding must be starting!"

"If we run, we can get this to Julia just in time," Kate said.

Only then did they take a good look at the veil. The fabric was rumpled and torn in one place. There were grass stains from the veil's tumble across the lawn. A few feathers clung to it, picked up from who knows where.

"There's no way we can give it to her like this!" Mia said.

"But there's no time left to fix it," Lainey said.

The tears welled up in Gabby's eyes again. Everything had gone wrong. She had spoiled Julia's perfect wedding. Worse than thinking about the trouble she'd be in was knowing how disappointed Julia would be.

chapter 9

The music woke Bess. At first, she didn't
know where she was. Then she spotted the
brown walls of her paper-bag prison. Her
stomach ached and her wings felt cramped.

Bess wiggled her fingers and toes to
wake them up. She was surprised to find
they moved freely. Where had her chocolate mittens gone?

Ugh, Bess thought. She'd eaten the
chocolate—every last bit of it. That
explained her stomachache.

The bag shook. Bess heard the boy shout, "Hey, that's *my* kite! What the— Oh my gosh!"

The bag suddenly dropped from his grasp. Bess couldn't flap her wings in time to stop herself from falling. She grunted as the bag landed in the grass. Bright light flooded in.

She could escape!

Bess dove toward the opening. As she fluttered out of the bag, she came face to face with the boy. When he saw her, his mouth opened so wide Bess could have climbed right inside it.

"A fairy!"

Before he could catch her again, Bess zipped away. She searched for a place to hide.

"Bess, up here!" a familiar voice called.

Bess looked up—and almost fell out of the air in shock. Her friends from Pixie Hollow were standing on the clubhouse roof. Prilla, Tink, Rosetta, and Dulcie were there, along with several other fairies.

"What are you doing here?" asked Rosetta.

"What are *you* doing here?" Bess replied in amazement.

"I came on a blink," Prilla replied. "I thought I'd just watch the wedding in secret, like you and I talked about. But then I saw the trouble. So I went back and brought everyone along to help."

Bess smiled at her friends. "You mean, you all came to rescue me?"

"Actually, no," Prilla said in surprise. "I didn't even know you were here. I meant Gabby. She's in trouble. We have to help her!"

*

When the fairies spotted the girls, they were trudging back toward the clubhouse. They held the ruined veil between them.

Bess overheard Gabby say, "What am I going to tell Julia?"

"Tell her you were playing with her veil when you shouldn't have been," Mia replied. "That's the truth."

"What's that fluttering sound?" asked Lainey.

The girls looked up as the fairies swooped toward them. When she saw all her Pixie Hollow friends, Gabby cried, "You came!"

"Everyone wanted to see you be a flower girl," Bess said.

Gabby's face fell. "Julia won't want me to be in her wedding. Not when she finds out what I did to her veil."

"That's why we're here," said Prilla. "Hand it over!"

Gabby did, and at once fairies set about fixing the veil. A sewing-talent fairy named Hem stitched up the tear. Her needle darted in and out so quickly it was a silver blur. A cleaning-talent fairy worked a bit of magic on the stains. Silvermist, a water-talent fairy, added dewdrops so the veil sparkled in the sunlight.

Meanwhile, the flower-talent fairies hurried off to collect petals from around the park. They filled Gabby's basket to the brim.

When Bess showed Dulcie what she'd done to the wedding cake, Dulcie threw her hands up in horror. Then she and the other baking-talent fairies set to work patching it up. They hid the dents Bess

had made in the frosting with little flowers they cut from strawberries.

In no time, everything was ready. The
only thing left to do was to return the veil
to Julia.

When Gabby knocked, the clubhouse
door flew open right away. Julia stood in
the doorway. "Did you find it?" she asked
eagerly. "Oh, girls, I thought you were Ms.
Cork. She's out looking for my veil. I don't
know where it's gone."

While Julia's back was turned, Bess
and the other fairies carried the veil in
through the open window.

"That's terrible," said Lainey, stalling.

"What does it look like?" Kate asked.

Julia frowned. "It's long and white and
it—well, it looks like a veil."

The fairies hung the veil on the hanger, then flew back out the window.

"You mean, like that?" Mia asked, pointing.

Julia turned just as the last fairy fluttered out. "Oh my gosh!" she exclaimed. "How did this get here?" She hurried over and lifted the veil from its hanger. "Want to help me put it on?" she asked the girls.

Of course they did. Kate and Mia helped fit the combs into Julia's hair, while Lainey and Gabby arranged the veil behind her.

"It looks different somehow," Julia said, examining herself in the mirror. "It's prettier than I remembered."

"You look even *better* than a princess," Gabby said.

Julia laughed. "I know it's just a piece of fabric. But something about it is special. Wearing a veil makes me *feel* like a bride. I guess that sounds silly, doesn't it?"

"No, it doesn't," said Gabby. "That's how I feel about my wings."

"Speaking of your wings, where *are* they?" asked Julia.

"Mami said I shouldn't wear them in the wedding," Gabby told her.

"But of course you can wear them!" Julia exclaimed. "They're part of what make you Gabby. Go put them on!"

If only she'd known sooner! "I can't," said Gabby. "They're at home."

"No, they're not," said Lainey. She unbundled the sweater she'd been carrying. There, to Gabby's amazement, were her beloved wings. "I took them from your room, just in case," Lainey explained. "It didn't seem right to leave them behind."

Gabby gave a little jump of joy. She slipped on the wings and sighed happily.

At that moment, Ms. Cork bustled into the room. "We can't wait any longer. The wedding should have started ten minutes ago! You'll have to get married without your— Oh, your veil!" she said when she saw Julia. "Where on earth did you find it?"

"It was right here after all," Julia said.

Ms. Cork gave a cluck of exasperation. Then she noticed the girls. "What are you all doing here? Hurry! Go find your seats! The wedding is starting!" She shooed Mia, Kate, and Lainey out of the room. "And Gabby, where did those wings come from? Take them off, please! It's time to start!"

"I told her she can wear them," Julia said. "I think they look perfect."

Ms. Cork threw up her hands. "Suit yourself. No one ever listens to the wedding planner." She hurried off, grumbling.

"Are you ready, Gabby?" Julia asked, taking her hand.

Gabby grinned and held up her flower girl basket. "I'm ready!"

chapter 10

The ceremony went by in a joyful blur for Gabby. Although Ms. Cork had told her to walk down the aisle slowly, Gabby skipped. She couldn't help it. She was so happy, it took all her effort to keep from floating away. When she thought no one was looking, she gave a secret little wave to the fairies, who were watching from a tree branch.

In the end, Gabby forgot to use fairy

dust on the flower petals, but it didn't matter. None of the guests seemed to pay much attention to the petals on the ground. Their eyes were on Julia. The bride looked dazzling as she came down the aisle, her veil dancing on a breeze that no one else could feel.

Later, under the big white tent, there was food and music and dancing. Gabby laughed when Julia and her new husband cut the cake and dabbed frosting on each other's noses. The cake turned out to be lemon with vanilla cream, and all the older girls agreed that Mia had won the bet, her guess being the closest. They were allowed to choose their own slices. Gabby picked the biggest she could find, one with extra strawberry flowers.

As she carried it back to the table where the other girls were sitting, she heard grown-ups in the crowd talking.

". . . just adorable. Those fairy wings were the perfect touch."

"Such a happy little girl. She looked like she was walking on air."

". . . those tiny flowers on the cake. How did they ever make them?"

"Did you notice the little footprints on top, as if the cake toppers were dancing?"

". . . such a beautiful bride . . ."

". . . such an elegant bride . . ."

". . . such a graceful bride. And that veil! I've never seen one like it."

Gabby smiled to herself. None of the grown-ups, not even Julia, would ever know how truly special the veil was.

Then Gabby saw Daniel hurrying toward her. "Gabby," he said urgently. "I saw you. You were flying, weren't you?"

Gabby didn't want to lie. But she didn't want to break her promise to Mia, either. She took a big bite of cake so she wouldn't have to answer.

"Don't worry. I won't tell. Can you teach me to fly?" Daniel asked.

"Mmm," said Gabby, chewing.

Daniel lowered his voice. "I saw a fairy here," he whispered. "I caught her. But she got away."

Gabby considered. If Daniel had already seen the fairies, then they weren't a secret anymore. Besides, she'd borrowed his kite. She wanted to do something nice for him in return. "Want to meet her?" she said.

"The fairy? You know her?" Daniel looked stunned.

"It's okay," said Gabby. "She's my friend. Come on."

Gabby led Daniel to a small round table in the very back corner of the tent.

Mia, Kate, and Lainey were already there, eating cake. In the middle of the table was a plate with another slice of cake. A dozen fairies sat around it.

If any of the grown-ups at the wedding had bothered to look closer, they would have seen the cake disappearing in itty-bitty chunks, as if being picked away by invisible hands. But Gabby knew grown-ups never thought to look for such things.

"This cake is quite tasty," Dulcie was saying as Gabby and Daniel walked up. "Not as good as fairy cake, but not bad at all. Bess, you should try some!" she called over to the art fairy.

But Bess was busy painting. She had stretched out a napkin on the table to use as a canvas, anchoring it with salt and pepper shakers. She glanced over at

Dulcie and made a face. "I think I've had enough sweets for one day."

Just then, Bess froze. She'd spied Gabby and Daniel.

"Hey, everybody," Gabby said. "This is my friend. His name is Daniel."

Daniel stared at the fairies. His mouth hung open a little. "Say hi," Gabby whispered to him.

"Hi," Daniel echoed, finding his voice at last. "I'm . . . um . . . sorry I put you in a bag. I thought you were a bug," he told Bess.

"Well." Bess sniffed, then gave a little nod to show she accepted his apology.

Gabby moved around the table to look at Bess's painting. Here was the bride with her dancing veil. And here was the groom wearing a goofy grin and Gabby throwing petals and all the guests in their nice clothes. Bess had even painted the fairies, though they were so tiny they looked more like butterflies.

"Look, Daniel. There you are," Gabby said, pointing. Bess had painted Daniel holding his little pillow with the wedding rings and a serious expression on his face.

"What are you going to do with the painting when it's done?" asked Mia.

"I haven't really thought about it," said Bess, who never bothered to do much with her art after it was finished. For her, making the painting was the best part. "I guess I could take it back to Pixie Hollow. Or you could have it."

Gabby looked toward the center of the tent, where Julia and her new husband were dancing. As Julia twirled, her veil floated out behind her, swaying in time with the music.

"I have a better idea," Gabby said. "Let's leave it with the presents. Julia will never know who made it!"

From across the room, a man called Daniel's name.

"That's my dad. I've got to go," Daniel said reluctantly.

"Daniel!" his father called again. "Come on!" He held up the dragonfly kite.

"We're going to fly my kite," Daniel told Gabby.

Gabby looked at Mia. "Can I go?" she asked.

"Sure, if Mami says it's okay."

Gabby hesitated. She wanted to go fly the kite. But she didn't want to leave her fairy friends. "Will I see you again soon?" she asked them.

"Very soon," Prilla promised.

"Until next time," Bess said, smiling.

Gabby grinned back. "Until next time," she said. Then she added in a whisper, "In Never Land."

Read this sneak peek of The woods Beyond, the next Never Girls adventure!

Lainey had never been deer riding without Fawn. In fact, she'd never been in the forest on her own. But that didn't stop her. Grabbing the harness, she ducked outside.

Just beyond the willow was a deer trail that led into the woods. Lainey followed it. At first it was slow going. The trail was no more than a matted-down path through the forest undergrowth. It disappeared in some places, only to pick up again in another spot. Sometimes Lainey wasn't sure she was following the same trail, or even following a trail at all. But the woods were quiet and peaceful, and it felt good to walk.

A bird whistled, and Lainey whistled back. She crossed a little stream, where silverfish flashed in the shallows. Lainey stuck her hand into the cool water and watched them scatter. A tiny frog, no bigger than a walnut, hopped along the bank. Lainey picked it up and cupped it in her hands, feeling its little heart beating.

As she set the frog back in the water, Lainey had the feeling she was being watched. Slowly, she lifted her head. A black-eyed doe was staring at her from behind the trees.

Her deer! Lainey jumped to her feet. The movement startled the deer and it darted away.

"Wait! Please wait!" Lainey cried, chasing after it.

The doe bounded down a slope. Lainey followed. But the hill was steep, and she lost her footing. The harness fell from her hand. She tumbled the rest of the way down and landed in a sticker bush.

"Oww!" Lainey tried to get up. But each little movement only made the thorns dig in more. She was stuck!

As she wondered what to do, she heard a voice say, "You're a pudding head!"

Lainey looked around, startled.

Through the leaves of the bramble she spied two red, pointed ears. They looked like the ears of a fox.

"If a bear and a lion got in a fight, the lion would definitely win," the voice went on.

"No way!" said a second voice. "I'm telling you, the *bear* would win."

Lainey shifted and caught a glimpse of a rabbit's fluffy white tail.

"Would not!"

"Would so!"

"Would not!"

An electric thrill went through her. All her life Lainey had wanted to talk with animals. She longed to know their feelings and thoughts. And here at last were two she could understand perfectly!